Also by Sheryl Noethe

The Descent of Heaven Over the Lake: Poems
(New Rivers Press, 1984)

Poetry Everywhere: Teaching Poetry Writing
in School and in the Community
(Teachers & Writers Collaborative, 1994)

Jumbo Love Cycle
(CD by The Stories Project, 1996)

The Ghost Openings

Sheryl Noethe

Grace Court Press
New York

The Ghost Openings

Library of Congress Cataloging-in-Publication Data

Noethe, Sheryl.
    The ghost openings / Sheryl Noethe.
        p. cm.
      ISBN 0-9702320-0-4 (alk. paper)
      I. Title.

PS3564.O33 G47 2000
811'.54--dc21

                        00-056203

Grace Court Press
375 Riverside Drive #5C
New York, NY 10025

Cover photo: Sheryl Noethe
Design: Chris Edgar

Printed by Draber Press, New York, N.Y.
Second printing

Table of Contents

THE LAST LAYER LIFTS

FROM A DARK COUNTRY PLACE

FJORDS

LOVE, SLEEP & PARIS

Dedicated to my lifelong companion,
Robert Jamshid Rajala

In memoriam
Clifford A. Rajala
1922–2000
"Never watch TV
without a book in your hands."

Ring the bells that still can ring
Forget your perfect offering
There is a crack in everything
That's how the light gets in.

—*Leonard Cohen*

A crack in the teacup opens
A lane to the land of the dead

—*W. H. Auden*

Fifteen apparitions have I seen,
The worst a coat upon a coat-hanger

—*Yeats, "The Apparitions"*

THE LAST LAYER LIFTS

ANTIMATTER

Astronomers discover a black hole in deep space
six hundred light years wide spewing a fountain of boiling antimatter.

It's like discovering a room in your house you never knew was there,
says the muscular newscaster, sparkling his dark eyes for the camera.
But I've dreamed about this room for years, imagining pathways behind
   the walls.

Antimatter. Sister to this globed and palpable world, lined up in lyric
   disorder.
More like not finding the room you never knew but spent your life in.
Un-being. Does it hurt? If I get it on my skin will I disappear?

Can it make me laugh? Is it heavier than stars?
Will it get me drunk, then spit me out? Will I shimmer like a rotted
   log?
So it eats daylight. Does it bounce and twirl or spill like milk?

Is it everything I am not? Does it lurk in a particle garden?
Why has it kept itself from us until now?
Can I compare it to the loss of love?

Could it be the soup of ghosts?
Does it run hot and cold?
Is it for sale?

Should we compare it to death?
Should we fear it?
Should we fear anything?

ARLENE

At the nursing home
I kiss her and walk
into the weak winter
sunlight on Nicollet Avenue.

When I lick my lips
I can taste the milk
she was drinking when
we said goodbye.

That butterfly in physics
moves its wings
and something happens
across worlds.

Always knowing that sweet milk was there.

EACH OF US AN IMAGE

First they said he jumped, then slipped,
   now he went swimming after a party.
      Walking the banks of the river with a friend.

Or a teammate. Depends upon who tells the story.
   All day I've felt them blasting the ice on the river.
      The drowned boy's body is hidden by death.

The nature of most of the universe
   Begs discovery.
      The dogs lift their noses to something on the air.

The demeanor of the dark matter
   is not certain.
      We only know it does not shine.

Now his father and brother,
   trapped in the prison house of sight,
      watch the men dynamite the locked-up river.

Wanting to find him afraid to find him
   looking for his hands not wanting to see them.
      His hair. Not wanting to see that yellow hair.

What about his clothes? Who will take them?
   A crowd has gathered. Someone is selling soft drinks from a cooler.

BY THE UPTURNED BOAT

The old woman fell, broke her hip and could not visit
her husband in the nursing home for almost a year.
When she finally arrived his body had grown scales,
like a fish, everywhere. She spent hours brushing them away.
Beneath the peel his skin was new.
He woke up, dull-eyed, and could not let go of her hand.
He could feel the lapping and the little tug almost stronger than air.
When, eventually, she left, he began wriggling backwards into the sand
beneath the blankets of the shore line
where the light bends
where the lost dog sleeps
where the dead child takes his first steps.

DONNA

These colors are wrong. Too wet.
　　Metal glints past this window and over the bridge.
Only the rage of light against nothing.

Now I am trying to avoid the falling places
　　That I did not know were here until you
Went down one of them.

Your head shatters inside mine.
　　I have no way to comprehend your violence.
These days since you are gone a drenched world

Jerks past too quickly.
　　Everything tainted with your blood.
The car, the ground, my thoughts.

Now you are a spirit in the bush.
　　No house to inhabit.
Only the mind can have you, re-forming the last minutes you left us.

Now certain trees are a delicate yellow-going-to-red
　　like prized Japanese peaches wrapped in wax as they grow.

Messages painted in kanji stain their skin: health, long life, children.
　　At the funeral your small daughters sang.

Little voices whispering about a bad dream and a gun
　　I will never wake to this color day without seeing a pistol in your
　　　grip.

Stark faces, briefly muted by confusion, half-expecting your return.
　　You will teach them what forever is. Hardly little girls now,

Proof that love is not enough. You are lost in an impulse too old,
　　Too wicked to refuse. Every day I ride up that road with you,
　　Donna.

And like the dead who return and have no voice, I beg you to wait.

Now you are queen and you are rain.
    No ears to hear the sorrow. A night of long dark.
Your youngest ran up to me, crying, Mama has run away and taken the
    gun.

Now your daughters will face the hard world of men without you.
    She cried in her sleep, said you came to her, rubbed her back.
Without hands. Under ground. Without hope. Over you bright
    Autumn
    Mourns.

All day long I forgot that you are dead.
    Until this afternoon, when a woman walked the edge of the road.
Dirt in my throat, brick and rust.

Deep Autumn. An impulse too old to resist.
    You had a dream and jumped out of it
By mistake.

How can death be more real? It has filled me with itself.

Now I see that I could not have stopped you.
    Last night was Halloween. We played at death with candy.
I lit candles in my window and along the path to my door.

You know who it is I was waiting for.
    Your ghost comes to my house and the dog shivers.
All wild-eyed and the world moves past us.

You are brooding in the truck, engine off.
    Clutching something in your handbag, knowing
This brief burst of energy and hope will not last.

A boy told me, years ago, that when he closed his eyes
    The world went black and fell away. He had no friends.
Who wants to be less than a shadow?

Your ghost is at the market, and in the low branches of the apricot tree.
    The dog lies on his back, whines and shudders.

I cut a green apple into quarters, slide my plate across the table.

I danced with your daughters at my wedding.
    From the wet grass butterflies circled our heads.
I have photographs where you are laughing.

That afternoon, gone. You closed your eyes, we went away.
    Now we live in the afterlife. I see you in the pink cheeks
        of the living.
I wonder if they know they are haunted so.

Over a week since your funeral. You are beyond forgiveness.
    I cry from deep inside the locked trunk of my body.
I am trapped, you are free.

I desire my slavery to this quickening.
    Every molecule a feast. Love and fear, all of it.
Maybe I can live with you inside and we can share my life.

I will find something beautiful. I'll say, Donna, look.

THE DEAD GO TO THE MOVIES

& sit on the laps of the living and suck
    at their lips like tomcats to babies.

They lick the milk off our mouths for us.
    They are sighing great musty sighs full of bad air.

They place their long noses along our necks and snuggle
    like puppies into our armpits and groins. They moan.

& we are laughing at the movie. *That's* what we believe in.
    What we had for lunch. The price of fixing the car.

The spirits continue swarming. They vomit diamond rings & snakes.
    They've rigged the basement with invisible pulleys and hoists.

No matter. Einstein says we can't see the future
    because the light cones are tipped in the wrong direction. Too bright.

We are the future's dead, dazzled.

GOODWILL THRIFT STORE, MISSOULA

It's hard to hate anyone
when we're all maybe trying on
the shoes of the dead together
trying on their slacks
and reading their books.
So we are gentle to each other
when we reach for the same
glass or blanket, smile when we collide
between the broken couch and a stain on the sheet.
We pass, cool ghosts who feel the sleeves
of jackets, the hems of dresses, and hold
nylon stockings up to the light.
An old man tries on a dead soldier's coat.
It weighs him down, he bends as though
he was carrying the man on his back.
When he opens his narrow pocketbook
a moth flies up.
We find blouses for our mothers
we never sent.
A past we never knew.
White bowls that fit inside each other.
Someone else's babies.
Painstakingly embroidered pillowcases.
Empty jars. Proof of happier lives.

When I pass the rack of dark wool suits
I smell a human musk, like an animal would.
I get the sense of a man, my long-dead grandfather,
and I am filled with love for the suits, love
for the man holding the double-boiler, love
for the teen-aged girl with bare feet, sucking
the ends of her hair and watching the clock,
love for the lonesome one who the shoes
will surely fit.

ARLENE AND I TRAVEL THE COSMOS

At first I was afraid it would burn me with friction;
        we flew up a narrow silver arc which fit just next to my skin
           at the chest
but I was not burned. And she was beneath my arm, I could see
        her frail white head her shoulders like the bones of a finch
          and we skimmed along the silver bar straight up.
Like sleepers we reached the top of the arc and kept going until
        we burst into an ocean of boiling white light;
          that's the only way to say it:
I felt no pain and she didn't weigh anything. We joined
        this motion, entered this brilliance as it entered us;
        I was filled with it;
          she was gone. I sat up in bed and looked at the clock, certain
Arlene was dead. Downstairs in the dark I called her husband
        who said she was with Faye in Texas. I called that number,
        Arlene answered,
          breathed my name. Whispered that Faye, best friend for sixty
years, former beauty queen, had just died in her arms. "Arlene, I saw her
to heaven."
        "No doubt," she said, then told me how she sat on the floor,
        her friend's body cooling in her lap, and finally
closed Faye's eyes. Since then she has promised
        that when she dies her soul will fly into my body.
        I wait for her.
        Once she dies, I will never be alone.

THE DREAM DOCTOR

1.
When I was a girl I burned the house down from my bed.
Firemen said it was the electric blanket.
I had been having the bad dream for years.
2.
Broken basement floor shooting geysers of thick oil.
It takes one spark, one crack in the wall where the dead look in.
3.
The head of a hammer with the horns of a goat.
The discovery that one is descended from Barbarians.
The mother who looks away, out the window, stares anywhere else,
says, what did you say honey.
4.
The poison bath. The unseen machine working in the cellar.
A door too heavy for a child to lift.
5.
Thirty years of pushing.
6.
Bleary thing in leg garters rolls over on the couch
and the five-year-old wakes up in animal fear for decades,
animating what lives in sleep: a basement with no door but a mouth,
arms that grow from walls with that unmistakable grip, outrageous size.
7.
Earthquake in the dream. Sidewalks buckle, downtown flattens.
I hang by my arms from a wobbly glass construction.
The hair of the doctor glints in the stained light.
A roaring wind sucks open both doors. A man walks toward me, then his
    head explodes.
8.
A helicopter crash-lands in the bed. A man falls out, body on fire.
I climb jagged sheet metal stairs to a broken telephone
    and keep dialing.
9.
It is four A.M. and I can hear a choir beneath the floor. The stove grins.
I have a hammer in my pocket and a baseball bat in the bed.
A tail-less black cat kills a rat in the attic. Something breaks free from the
    furnace

and sprints up the stairs. Gripping my pinking shears, I wonder how
   the material
object can defeat the metaphysical terror. I am too big for the hamper,
   too big
for under the bed. I am overtaken with the proportional void.
10.
I was waiting in the coffin for Popeye and Brutus. Abe Lincoln directed
traffic on the road to hell. Some things I do not know if they happened.
   Was it a dream?
11.
The mattress in the garage. The fire. He denied everything.
12.
The babysitter is afraid of the uncle who drops by when he has been
   drinking.
He takes out his false teeth and we scream and hide our faces.
13.
Afraid of grown ups, of drunk people and parties.
   Something happened.
On the stairs. I remember the sound.
14.
Distinctly afraid anyone alone with her will initiate a sexual act.
15.
Robbed of my sensuality, said the woman.
Something missing in our love, said the husband before he disappeared.
16.
In my diagram spirit sits next to sex. The most direct route to one
is through the other. The man was draped over my back and forced
   himself
into my future. His breath on my neck, his bad language, and then I
   was
trying to pry myself outside of my body.
17.
An unspoken agreement not to recognize him. A constant peripheral
   blur.
18.
Out of the corner of my eye, a man attacking. A dog with bared fangs.
I am organizing information in order to stay alive.
19.
I don't have to love him. I can overwhelm him.
He drinks and finds me beneath contempt, he says.

20.
Like the grandmother who died in childbirth,
I have barely survived the love of the family.

THE LONELINESS OF MY BROTHER

1.

This is the loneliness of my brother.

Today I saw a woman sitting alone laughing at what she held in her
glass.

My brother laughs behind a closed door alone in a room.

This is the loneliness of my brother. I dreamt we quarreled.

I picked him up and beat him against a brick wall until all that was left
was a pair of pants.

This, too, is the loneliness of my brother. I dreamt he was a boy, drunk,

laughing and stumbling against me. I held him in my hands. He became
a rabbit made of ice.

I dropped him on the sidewalk and he melted into a pool of water.

How, I asked, can I tell our mother?

I see him in the faces of transient men.

I see him in the fearful eyes of boys.

I see him in my eyelids and muscles.

I understand he is almost entirely alone.

Imagine the loneliness of living on in the dream of your sister.

A rabbit of ice, a pair of empty pants.

I understand almost nothing about him. He keeps secrets.

The only time he wants to talk about anything personal is when he's
drinking.

Our last conversation he asked me if I'd considered suicide.

This from the man who gets a pistol in his hand and plays roulette.

Passes out on his desk at work with the gun in his grip.

Police break down the door. Everyone thought he was dead.

Lay on my parent's bed shooting holes in the walls and ceiling.

This is the loneliness of the one who laughs alone.

The woman looked like my brother, propped on the street reverend's
arm,

faded tatoos, red lips and blonde straggled hair. So pleased with everything

she laughed herself cross-eyed . Pulled way inside and shrunk into a
ball.

On a shelf called emotion stands a frozen figure. Vomiting smoke.

Something flies into my house. Black feathers drift.

I call the dogs in and go looking.

In the silence of the fiddle head and forsythia I look for the body.
Broken neck, I imagine. Tiny bones, eggshell skull. But nothing is there.
My mother told me that a bird flying into a window is a harbinger of
    death.
A black bird, she said, will throw itself at your house.
I used to fight for intervention and de-tox. Now I only wait.

     2.

All I know is the summer went by.
Suddenly the leaves are reddening.
Ran into a local poet who referred
to this suddenness and deepening
as *the August singularity* then he
snaked his arm around my waist &
grinned.
Next night the meteorologist refers
to these brisk evenings as the *third
week anomaly* while I wonder if my
tomatoes will succeed at presenting
killer fruit red as shark's happiness.
The fair is over.
That black and white cat is back at
the gate. She makes herself flat and
slips underneath. Two big dogs live
at my house. She will risk her life for
curiosity.
Or maybe something winged lies hurt
in my deep grass.

HALF-HEAD

Cranial vasoconstriction precipitated by irritability and rage.
    Massive slow potential deep within the brain
radiates to open the gates of pain within the spine.
    Visual tumult, delirium in which latticed, faceted and tesselated motifs
      predominate.

I lie on the cool wood floor beside the chair. My little dog comes over
    to rest his head on mine. He forces his nose into my neck and shudders.
Medicine dog. I count my pulse by explosions in my temple.
    Small animals chase back and forth and insects march on the edges.

Five days pass where landmines behind my eyes respond to light.
    Scintillating scotoma, bright swallowed by dark.
Launched by expanding phosphenes, and geometric spectra.
    Implicit in the cerebral repetoire from spinal horn
    to brainstem formation.

Innate resonance mechanism on the borderlands of epilepsy.
    Ascending bombardment of the cortex, which responds with activity of
      its own.
In the emergency room I hold my head in my hands in dark glasses.
    The nurse walks in with the secret to my well-being.

The needle explodes beneath my shoulder and closes my throat.
    My limbs burn. Heat rises into my head. Lie down, she says,
    wait for it to work.

> "First the beating of the heart was felt,
> then it seemed to become audible as sound
> two lights appeared before the eyes . . .
> the figure of an old woman in a red cloak
> who offered something that had the smell of
> Tonquin beans"
>
> —Oliver Sacks, *Migraine*

Slowly my throat opens. The burn ceases and the great gong of my skull is still.
    I do not have the nightmare that leaves the bad feeling. I do not listen
to the first bird as the grey rises. Head sore as a basketball, I walk through the
    house
    like I am walking on ice. I do not make any sudden moves.

The great bruise of my head is restful. There is no echo.
    Get a needle of your own, the nurse tells me. She mimes a hand
releasing a plunger into her thigh. When the headache comes
    shoot this into your leg.
    It closed my throat, I tell her. Only for a while, she says.

I was afraid, I say, that I would die.
    Yes, she says, but the question is, isn't it worth it?
The visual outskirts boil over with tumultuous light.
    Particular symptoms to which particular symbolic values are attached.

Dynamic patterns illuminate the substrate of the mind to organize and destroy.
    In the form of hallucinatory display an entire self-organized system
of universal behavior holds not only the secrets of the neurons deep within the
    brain
    but the creative heart of nature itself.

I run my mind over the roof of my head like a tongue at a tooth, wondering
    where did the headache go, and for how long?
I am like a man who survives an airplane crash and walks out of a bloody cornfield.

WHEN HE FELL

Joe landed on his head he went a little crazy on the ice by the forty-second
    street dairy
at first he seemed all right but a blood clot pushed on his brain he began to
    believe Arlene
was paying my rent and sending regular checks to her sister
he said my dad was skimming
ten percent off of all roofing work done in the city
and then he claimed my Aunt Donna was pouring
battery acid on his cucumber patch.

He bought locks for all the doors and outside gates. No one went in no one
    came out.
One night he dragged her down the basement stairs by her arms on her knees
    she was
eighty-three he pushed her over to the wall
where the plaster was chipping to show
where my dad was tunneling beneath the house. Later she found the foodstuffs
    he'd hidden away—cans of sardines, chocolate, soup, milk powder, cigars.

The gentle neighbor who used to invite my dad to stop in for a cold one
now looked at us with contempt. He asked my mother if she'd worked out the
    deal to sell his heart.
Finally his son went to court to declare Joe incompetent.
His mind weakened his heart grew stronger. His last years spent in the nursing
home, in the wheelchair, drugged and dismantled, heart pounding like a bull's.

She was there the night he died. She scratched at the scales growing over his
    skin where no one had touched him.
She took his hand, said, It's okay, daddy, okay to let go.
She fell asleep with her head on his bed, still holding his hand. His soul lum-
    bered out of him like an eagle heavy with kill.
It flapped in confusion and sorrow, ever so slowly,
out of the wheelchair out of the nursing home out of the broken skin.
When she woke up he was gone without looking back, big heart still.

FROM A DARK COUNTRY PLACE

BEST SEEN FROM A DARK COUNTRY PLACE

Corner house on Elm, blue with a black roof. Walk past it. Close your
    eyes.
In the after-image you can see the later Rothko paintings.
    Nothing left but rectangles.
Color itself, he said, *is reason enough.*

Here where there are no city lights to compete with the skies
you can watch meteor showers go whizzing across August.
Best seen, they say, from a dark country place.

Just like this, says my guest, a dark night, dogs reclining like lions.
A train wails. My pup rests his head on my open palm in the grass.
There hangs the Rothko, framed by leafy branches.

However you paint the larger picture, you are in it.

He later requested his paintings be shown only in dim light.
Earth's light, smudged and failing.
Figures lose value. Form disappears. All that's left
is the drama of the mind. Gradually purging the canvas of memory,

history, and geometry. *Obstacles*, he called them,
    between the painter and the idea.
That summer on Clinton Street the sky tore open in thelocyanide blue
and the secrets of form were outlined in a nervous green light.
Expanding and quickening in the eyes. Not the farther but the nearer shore.

We walked the yard, picking up kimonos that fell from us the night
    before like sighs.
Don't you have these colors in your life, stained until canvas and pig-
    ment are one?
Fleeting glimpses of underpainting, repeated washes until the effect is
    of a hidden source of light.
A maximum luminosity where all colors hover at the same plane.

Rothko finally found the human figure impossible for his own use.
Instead, his color field, the glowing activity between tones.

The sorrow of this later work helps me understand the light here in
    these very circumstances.
The yellow rectangle floating over blue taped to my kitchen wall was for
    a while the only way to imagine any future at all.

Specific references to beach, sea and sky are unnecessary.
The way water holds the scent of the otter who swam past the day
    before
my dog puts his face in the river, closes his eyes, and inhales.

THE APPROACH TO CHALLIS, IDAHO

October in the Pahsimeroi
    These hills are forbidding and voluptuous
        Circus animals escaped from an upended train.

Round brown elephants sprawl cattywampus
    While camels roll beneath a blanket of soil.
        The luxury of a line of color

Breaks to reveal a stone ache of color
    Scrubbed and parched rainshadow pallor
        Interrupted now by human language.

Ten Mile Creek says a road sign
    Up The Creek Creek
        Elk Bend Sports Lodge

Ten miles from where? I wonder.
    The road curves like a liar's story
        Talus slope glittering ebony behind me.

In the rearview mirror the yellow tunnel of October closes
    Small explosions of oxblood in the willows
        Stained walls of the canyon fold where water has cut like a knife.

Warning signs appear, illustrations to suggest
    The next ten miles will be like a drunk man on thin ice.
        In a steep shadow I follow one bend around another.

Obedient to the road, attentive as a new bride.
    Finally the valley opens up before me, and the town of Challis perches
        On an alluvial fan at the throat of the Salmon River Range

Sparkling like peeling aluminum rooftops, rusted chrome
    and an abandoned gold mine.

FIRE

1.

At first when we met
    the fireman was the rock
        and I was the fireworks.
Then, as we stayed together over the years,
    he became more firework-like and I more rock-like
        just watching the world go sparking past.
Catching a few words here and there
    forming a slow thought until the distinction between
        firework and rock became mere semantics.

2.

Candle flickering beneath curtain.
    Curling iron fallen between cushions.
        Heating pad cooking under the blanket.
            Cigarettes in the fingers of the sleeping.
A woman runs toward a crib, her long hair on fire.
    The fireman steps into his clothes and is out the door.
        While he is gone I dream the mirror is aflame.
            He looks for the new shape beneath the ash.
Nothing disappears completely, he assures me.
    Layer by layer what remains represents the original composition.
        Christmas presents wrapped beneath the tree.
            A pile of laundry beside the water heater.
Where a blue flame twitches, itches to trace its finger
    along invisible lines to the flannel pajamas.
        Metal and glass lean to point where the fire began.
            It's still all here, disguised and oxidized.
The way rust takes a car. One hundred years, a lifetime,
    in a moment. I walk into the rooms of the poem
        where I have never been like a man walks into a burning house
            searching for the hidden source of light.

THE PRINCIPAL

For Jerry McVay

I walk past the school and look at his window
he is watering a plant and does not look up
he holds the pitcher in his large hands
as gently as he holds a weeping child.
At the end of the day, toward dusk
the halls of the building are strangely silent
and the empty floors shine like ghostly souls.
Last week he took a hand grenade from a student
brought for show and tell
ran it out to his car, cupping it like an egg.
None of us knew if it was live
and we held our breath
waiting for the worst.
He is a tall man with long legs.
He bent over what he held
as though to absorb the force
within himself
keeping us safe from the war.
He would go into a home full of drunken uncles
to get a boy to class on time
He says, catch your breath and tell me slowly.
Let me see if I can help.
Sometimes at night when I pass
I see the blue light of his computer
reflected like a watch fire on his face.

RURAL POETRY WORKSHOP

I could hear them screaming from the spelling bee
and it made me uneasy, suggesting a tension that pushed
at the surface, pouching into a weakening wall, a dike ready to give.
The drummer told me he couldn't sleep thinking about this day,
worried that he wouldn't be interesting enough, that he'd bore the kids,
that he might get a bad name, never be asked back, that sort of thing.
Look, I said, you're an artist. If there's a wild card anywhere it's the kids.
They're worked up and it's hot and they've eaten lots of candy.
The parents will leave to go chat in the hall, and the teachers decide it's not
        their job . . .
I could see I was making things worse so I shut up.
The hundred and forty arrived, looking at us like they already suspected
we would try our best to dupe them.
I took half the group to a classroom for the poetry workshop where they
        revealed
not a pencil or sheet of paper among them, not a care in the world.
They sat down and eyed me warily.
I walked among them, describing how to assemble a chant poem,
        one line per student.
Describe yourself as a part of nature, as a color, a movement, a sound.
The first boys refused, just shook their heads
        and settled farther into their hats.
They had no idea my desperation was so much greater
        than their desire not to speak.
I grinned hard, sweating, heart-beat rustling in my ears, and moved in closer.
Inches from each face I asked where they found their favorite color,
        what machinery they could master,
        what animal they spied upon. I figured it could go two ways.
Either I could engage them with the force of my will
        and sheer rocklike wall of faith
or it could all break down, we would reveal
        that there was no connecting luminous
umbilicus between us, that language holds no contract, that one generation
simply waits for the last to die, that entropy rules a formless sea.
We reassembled for a poets' chorus accompanied by the drummer's rhythm,
        bells & chimes.
I divided them into two groups and walked child to child with the
        microphone.

One boy described himself as a deer drunk on beer. Another was a blistering badger

crawling through the tunnel gap. The flight of owls and hawks. The red of a tractor.

The moon on the wood beneath your bare feet on a night when you cannot sleep.

We finished in record time. The teachers lined up their students to climb back on the buses

and get home to chores, thankfully free of poets begging for images.

The drummer and I collapsed on the stage floor and I said,
    chaos wanted to touch us.

It reached for us from behind the air. I could smell it. That's why you couldn't sleep.

You had a premonition that chaos knew your name
    and in the group of children
    it would lay its hand upon you.

I helped him load his drums into the car. He said I made a good roadie.

It was mid-afternoon and we were free.

    The road stretched ahead like an uncurling ribbon.

We sped back to our lives. Chaos followed like a faithful dog.

AFTER ROBERT PINSKY'S SAMURAI SONG
(After Ms. Rose's 4th Grade)

Here is the formula, I said to the children,
When I had no blank I made blank my blank.

I did not talk about loss to the 4th grade, or inevitability.
The brown-eyed boy said, *When I had no food I made hunger my feast.*
The slow girl who never raises her eyes wrote, *When I had no lunch I made the
snow my soup.*
Flakes the size of handkerchiefs tossed themselves at the windows.
Her friend, also in the slow row, had her own take on the arrangement.
I am my cat princess. I am my brother carl with red hair
When I lean over her to spell a word, my eyes find
her tiny fingernails bitten to the quick, her torn and bloody cuticles.
She and the slow girl are kind to each other because no one else has time
When I had no house the bridge was my bed.
They walk behind the other kids at recess. The small one writes about her
grandpa, who gets her breakfast and brings her to school. She has drawn
a collection of dogs in various sizes and given them to me. Once I heard
the teacher call her Peanut and ruffle her hair. I called up a sudden love.
When I had no water I made air my drink.
When I had no sleep I made the dark my mystery.
When I had no friends, I made daydreams my companions.
When I have no happiness, I am satisfied with my sadness.
They like when I give them rather elaborate forms
which they memorize and use again, long after I have forgotten.
They know it is essential to draw a picture when the writing is finished.
The day is exhausted when I climb to the second floor and teach poetry
to another group of 4th graders, these in particular wild and chaotic.
When I had no mind I made the wind my imagination.
They like to shock each other, make the whole class gasp, hands over mouths, eyes
round. Out-of-control body functions make good closure for these poems.
Because I had no arms I made flowers my hands.
And then, from the back of the room in a corner, a stringy little voice
and big glasses, cowlick, organic events ongoing in desk, patches
of things attaching and falling away, huge pencils manipulated across the tundra
of the empty page:
When I had no light I made the darkness my lantern.

LUMINOUS OVER THE JUNKED CARS

It starts like this: Last night I dreamt again of the man I once loved & I
    loved him again.
It really starts like this: Because my mother could not love me I adopted
    another family.
In 4th grade I ran a good 60-yard dash and became a fast girl. The girl I beat
    befriended me. She whispered that I could marry her brother and we
    would be sisters.

It started behind the wheel of a red bike with a loose chain
where I sat on the corner watching his window for most of my adolescence.
She read Einstein to me aloud, quoting that God does not play dice with the
    universe,
I found one of her brother's long yellow hairs in my underpants and knew
    we were meant.
I stepped off a greyhound bus on the shoulder of a road in South Dakota
crossing a broken field in city shoes, a fiend carrying her suitcase toward a
    light

on a front porch; a long yellow man and a chicken-killing dog inside.
Just last night I dreamt his eyes were as yellow as a lion's.
Dreamed South Dakota a drunken drive away.
I woke addled with loss over something he said

in a pizza parlor twenty years ago. Nights the Northern Lights
    lit the field of sky, luminous
over the junked cars while we took turns
    shooting his gun from his bed.
I chased him from childhood on bike, bus & barstool,
    watching the windows of his houses.

I dreamt that he didn't cut off his hair, didn't get rid of the dog.
It's all momentum and entropy; inescapable laws in a tossed salad,
barometic pressure and ricochet, his electrons flying into space
due to torque and inflection while I was flipped eight-ways-to-market
in the opposite direction: no underlying plan, no intent, and I am broken
    here crushed by my belief.
To summon him in sleep, to wake and live with grief.

MIRAGE

The man in the Mexican Restaurant had your build.
Your haircut, shoulders, rib cage and behind.
You, easy. From the back, in a minute.
My body, turncoat, began agitating.
Warm, welcoming sensations.
Cling peaches in heavy syrup.
Entirely consumed by you.
Until, as mystery will,
he turned his head to reveal
a stranger. The wrong man.

If only
he could have stood still
with his back to me
forever.
Just like you.

UNIS VERSUM

Reverie before sleep embodies the past.
      Ghost rumbling through the kitchen.
The DNA footprint of your cells
      Could be drawn from the inside of my embrace.
Cooling now, but proof.
      Lights flicker. Dog dreams of rabbit.
Husband says a word from sleep.
      Sleep, where universes intersect.
Where half a country and twenty years
      do not mean or matter.
This turn we take together,
      the language of line drawing.
The A that was once an oxen, dog leaping at the tree,
      paws curled like faux wings
in the sign for angel.
      Say you dream of a man for years.
These dreams leave you full of love.
      What is the word for it? I need this word.
A molecule split open and entered.
      My body, which cannot lie, which is chained
to the truth of childhood, age and illness,
      is completely convinced.
Each dream of you, as real as this.

DECADE

Those cool Manhattan
mornings still blue
sidewalks we rose
before the sun
turned the city
to an oven
and drove your father's
garbage truck up
the Hudson River where
you dropped me off on
94th and Amsterdam
where I slept for
an hour or so in my room
before taking the train
up to the Bronx where I
urged school children to
remember their dreams &
talk to animals
while you drove over
the bridge to New Jersey
to work the route
on the big truck
with your father
while waiting for the break
you need to take
your band on tour
with the Fleshtones
and be on MTV
never imagining how
money and travel would
turn your heart to booze
and cocaine
how you would nearly destroy yourself
in your bigger life while I
grew gradually nearly too tired
to stay alive and moved to
Idaho to teach mountain kids
to trust completely in the

imagination while I
learned to drive a stick shift,
chop wood, bank a fire,
and surround myself
with dogs and children
and once or twice
I saw you on t.v.
and saw your face
on tapes in stores
and I remember you
in your underwear
on the Lower East Side
in a room
where the former tenant
had stenciled skulls and crossbones
with ink so indelible
it soaked slowly through
every layer of paint
you ever put over it
and your pointed Beatle boots
stomping out the beat so hard
the whole stage shook
as I shifted my life
in thirteen cardboard boxes
out of Washington Heights
to the West where I had
the good luck to meet
a brave fireman and move in
and once we saw you
on t.v. and I
didn't say
a word.

THE DREAM MAP

Last night Arlene drew a map to show the abyss between speaking and
  silence,
a sort of landscape with a deep blue body of water
  between green continents.
When she was failing, lying in the nursing home talking to the dead,
I took a bath at her house.
There, beside the tub, lay one of her narrow brown barrettes.
I took it. Every day I have worn it in my hair, which I am growing long.
After my dream about the map I wore the dress with the trapeze skirt that
  she made me.
I remember the hot July day she took my measurements,
  inch by inch, patting me all over.
Then she sized her dressmaker's dummy to fit me.
I look now at the hem of the dress and see the tiny white Xs,
  her hand's stitches,
so precise, so evenly spaced.
Even though I lived a thousand miles away, in her sewing room she
  could have my form.

PASSION

Today my husband sandbagged Pattee Creek.
Spring run-off and all the rain caused floods.
When school let out he carried children
Across the rushing water.

When I was five our school flooded.
Firemen in yellow slickers
Carried us from the classroom.

When he tells me about his day
I am a child lifted over rising water
By a man she does not know
And set upon higher ground.

I embrace him, say, *Hero*
and he's embarrassed, his face colors.
I like this work, he tells me.
That's all he wants to say.

The minute I met him I remembered
How he helped me fly to dry land
A long time ago and I have been looking for him since.

THREE TRUE ACCOUNTS

HUSBAND

Has a bumblebee in the middle
    that hums in the mouth of the woman who pronounces it gladly.
        The first half of the world is a loose woman
           or small sewing kit.

Hussy. Husband. Correlative of wife. Tiller of the ground.
    Hus, house. Bunda, head. This house has a bee in its bonnet.
    This house has a wood floor. Those are my hips.

My head I will have for a little table. A husband lives in my hand.
    Up the long stairway to the turret. A round, windowed room.
        A tiny sink with real water. His warmth, his press, his fit

against my body. I wake to find the bear, the stranger in the boxcar,
    the sound of someone walking through tall sunflowers,
        all changed now back into the husband.

DEVIL

Comes, like ballistic and diabolic, from diabolos,
    slanderer. Diabolos, a throwing across your path.
        Bolos, that hard wooden ball, thrown

on a summer picnic, that comes into sightline
    and then hits your head.
        He takes your soul. As quick as that.

HELL

A hidden place, like kel, which covers.
    Also follows apocalypse, to uncover.
        Cell and cellar, two small rooms.

Conceal and helmet. Also, pod, hull, occult, color & holster.
    Hell is a hall. Hall has a roof
        Hell has six feet of dirt. That's all.

DENTAL ILLNESS

The Life of a Tooth.
The sad truth of the life of a tooth is forty years, more or less.
A friend who worked as a hygienist once told me, wistfully,
that your teeth are the only set of pearls you are given.

My father was too poor as a child to go to the dentist. His first visit
was while he was in the army.
    That dentist butchered my father's mouth.
My father passed out in the chair. From then on, any dentist,
    any chair, he fainted.
I remember all the teeth pulled slowly from the front of his smile.

Childbirth
The most common comparison to dental work is childbirth;
    the hours of labor, the intense pain, the inevitable extraction.
    Kidney stones also fill this bill,
an exquisite pain, bloody urine, something large
    passing through something small.

My father worked in the spray paint booth of Ziegler Auto Body.
Our dentist's name was also Ziegler. I became confused:
sanding, buffing, cavity, putty, dent, filling, and so on.
I had too many big teeth for my mouth, a fact of evolution.
Ziegler, the dentist not the auto body shop,
    pulled my eye teeth, my canines.

My Mother told me the enamel on our teeth was weak.
She did not see a dentist until she was pregnant with me
when she lost two teeth to build my fetal bones.

In a downtown club in the District of Columbia
    I met a military dentist, a captain, who suggested we go to his office
    and take laughing gas, then go at dawn Sunday morning
to the cathedral and get flogged.
We drove to his operatory and strapped on the laughing gas masks.
    We laughed and laughed. The air was a thin blue odor.

He looked at my teeth. I laughed. The metal tip of his explorer
    broke off in my molar.
This date is over, I cried. He said, think of it as a free filling.
    Ten years passed.

My husband convinced me to see a children's dentist with a waiting
    room full of toys
and prizes. Haltingly I described the events that led to the dental tool
    bit in my jaw.
I was afraid the new dentist would drill on it and the metal bit would
    explode into my brain.
He took X-Rays. The bit had fallen out at some point and I'd likely
    swallowed it.
He didn't ask any specific questions about the military dentist, like,
    did we go to the cathedral and get flogged?

At forty my teeth went to hell. Root canal. I'd compare it to exquisite
    medieval torture.
One of my tangled roots pierced my sinus. Off to the emergency ward
    for two shots
of demerol in my butt. The demerol lodged in little pockets of serum
    that hurt like hell
if jiggled. It's hard not to jiggle one's behind.

One winter while auditing a class on women poets
something crashed in my mouth like agonized glaciers. I discreetly
    pulled out a little triangle of tooth. My dentist later told me my
    many crooked teeth were on a collision course. Never should have
    let Ziegler, auto body specialist, pull the eye teeth, thus unmooring
    my upper jaw like a harbor full of drunken boats.

At the Jazz Bar in suburban Minneapolis a convention of dentists recre-
    ates. I am standing
at the cigarette machine when one of them leans into the cobalt neon
    and looks into my face.
Looking thunderstruck, he tells me how very odd my lacking eyeteeth
    make my smile.

The Evil One, my endodontist, told me his patients don't need pain
medication. Said something about the golden age of dentistry and
the gates of pain in the brain. I should have listened to the little
voice warning me. My jaw trembled convulsively. He responded
with a bite block. Afterward I wrote him an unfriendly letter listing
in detail his human folly, his hubris.

A tooth was drilled upon at length. It was an old tooth and it died.
In my mouth.
While shooting serum into my jaw hinge the dentist made a friendly
suggestion: couldn't I find a poem in all of this?
I mean, look at Dante.

During the root canal itself I was able to listen
to all four sides of a two-tape best hits of Aretha Franklin.
After emptying the roots of my tooth of their living pulp
he filled the echoing canals with liquid rubber, which he shot out of a
sort of glue gun. Here's the best part, though:

At the Halloween party, I went as a starlet. Dressed in the wig and
heels and mole and stole I'd like to wear for everyday. Black silk
scarf over my platinum and purple cat's eye sequin sun-glasses.
Nobody knew me. Toward the end of Halloween night a disco guy
and a witch showed up. He had tight bellbottoms platforms body
hair Rod Stewart wig open polyester shirt. . . .

Somebody called him the dentist. It was the guy who would perform
the upcoming root canal.
I managed to get introduced. Wobbling in Italian spike heels I explained
about Walter Reed Military and the Evil One and my dad, who's had all
of his teeth yanked.

I wrote this poem for my dentist, for the emergency room doctor who
shot me up with novocaine at 4 a.m. for the writer who rolled up
her dog's babytooth in bread and ate it, for the mysterious life of
the tooth with its root and canals and its likeness to a pearl.
I wrote this poem primarily, I now see, for Arlene. Here is her story:
I have a tooth that never descended. It causes a small gap in my smile.
My dentist wanted to pull it down for cosmetic reasons.
Before I got married he offered to file my teeth into a straighter line.

I've chipped each of my front teeth many times on bicycles, on a ring,
on a light chain, upon landing. When I told Arlene he wanted to pull
   that tooth down, she said, Leave it where it is. If you ever lose
   another tooth, that one will track over and replace it.
I gave this information to my dentist. She's ninety-three years old,
I said. My tooth will track over. My mouth will be saved.

Now for the question of medieval people. How did they survive? If this
   is the golden age of dentistry, why do dentists have
the most suicides? Is it true that a good surgeon might
   also have made a good butcher?
Here's how I now understand the medieval people.
They were lucky enough not to live to forty, the life of a tooth,
   more or less.

AN ATTEMPT TO DESCRIBE BEATRICE

1.

We got her out of the sanitarium where she learned to cheek her pills.
She got out of the marriage to Larry. The night before she left
she brought coffee and lit cigarettes
    in two ashtrays for my mom and dad.
They sighed and looked like something had been gotten through.
That night she cleared out my closet and disappeared;
all my Carnaby Street hip-hugger skirts, chain belts,
granny purses, loud floral orange and yellow shirts.
She was my aunt but we wore the same size.
    We didn't hear from her for six months.
Then my Aunt Geraldine called to say Beatrice turned up
in Oklahoma City, bruised, broke and redeemed.

2.

Years later, after she married the banker and begin raising
Rhodesian Ridgebacks and German Shepherds I asked her
about that time, when she stole my clothes and ran away.
She left the guy that beat her up on their honeymoon.
She went with two men to California in a stolen car.

3.

Her mother died when she was five then she slept with her dad.
He entered her in beauty contests and dressed her up.
She discovered men and he disowned her.
After she was seventeen she never saw her father again.

4.

They held up gas stations all the way to L.A.
No, she was only the driver. She never held the gun.
They financed their return trip the same way but something
went sour between her and one of the men. She jumped out
of a moving car in Oklahoma, picked the gravel out of her hands
and hitch-hiked to her sister Geraldine's.

5.

After that she dated only policemen.

6.

She had a little dog she called Capezio.
She could lasso a man from afar with her cobra eyes.

She could draw him toward her like a curling vapor of smoke.
Later she became an atheist who raised talking birds.

7.
She had some children with the police.
    One guy did something or other,
she cut up his shoes and uniforms into two-inch squares,
piled them in the hallway outside their door.
She had a baby that died in her womb.
She lived in housing projects just north of the city.
Her boy up and nailed all of his toys to the bedroom wall,
drove lines of nails to balance his rubber balls.
Her girl hid in the laundry room instead of going to school.
As a child this daughter called every man daddy.
She inherited my aunt's unfortunate taste in men.
They lived in mobile home lots the size of small towns.

8.
I went with my aunt for alcohol rehab.
    We almost ran off with our cabbie on our way.
We learned together about A.A.
She cleaned houses then learned to build them.
When I was a child I was afraid of her parties and her boyfriends.
She gained and lost hundreds of pounds;
    carried a six-pack wherever she went.
Most of the police who stopped us had dated her and quickly let us go.
The baby that died in her womb was induced.
The hospital staff said only her husband could be with her.
    I said I was him.

9.
She borrowed a cop's car and threw it from forward
to reverse, smashing cars in front of and behind her.
She turned on the siren and red light.
    We stood on our front lawns and watched her,
the antics of her boyfriend the policeman as he ran alongside his car.
    She was a ball. We were all of us afraid of her.
In treatment, she was smarter than the doctors.
Funnier, too, she could wrap her gaze around a man
    and make him blind.
She liked danger, men who could spin basketballs on their fingers.
Then she married the banker. Once in a while she ran away.

She and her daughter dated together.
    Her daughter's boyfriend went to jail.
The banker bought her more dogs, then birds;
huge cages of intelligent blue parrots with eighty-year lifespans.
The big dogs moved outside.
The daughter's lover got out of prison and she moved back in with him.
The grandson tore all the heads off of his toys.

10.
I miss her. We had a falling out in a bar around Xmas.
She wanted to go home with the band. A friend and I
dragged her to our car. She hasn't spoken to me in years.
I remember her little dog Capezio, so tiny she could carry
him in her purse.

DIAGNOSTIC

1. Early Twenties
I dreamed kittens were stuck to my sweater.
When I pulled them away their sharp claws snagged in the yarn.
I was pregnant. The kittens *adhered.*

2. Thirties and Beyond
My own blood spilled from me and then stuck to my legs.
I told the acupuncturist. She told me she wished her boyfriend
would desist from pork. She said the Chinese called what I had *sticky blood.*

3. The Indeterminate Dream
I was visiting a friend. I went into the dark bathroom where
I stood in ankle deep liquid and when I put the light on,
my own blood was everywhere. It drenched a small, round rug.

4. The Quality of Pork
My acupuncturist put the needles in and sometimes forgot to take them out.
Once I found one in my hairline at the Credit Union. She said her boyfriend
was still eating ham. *It's nearly human,* she said.

5. Taste
I dream I am moving into a disgusting apartment in New York.
As I move a pile of rags from the floor a nest of baby cockroaches
flies up into my mouth. It leaves a bad taste I cannot brush away.
It becomes influenza over the course of a day.

6. Pygmies and the Midwestern Proportional Void
There were the dreams of misproportions. *My hands were too big to be real.*
You know this one. *My head swelled to fit the bed.* Familiar yet? When I
    had a fever
I was like a jungle dweller who stands on a cliff and sees an antelope
    across the plains,

7. and he believes
that he can hold the animal in two fingers. He believes what he sees.
I used to think when I closed my eyes, everything actual disappeared.
    All that remained
was a furious vacuum, all blackness, and me at the center of it.

8. The Body

The body will tell you the truth in images you'll barely remember, shadows across the brain, unstable memory, wit's end prophecy.

The way your body spoke to you before the world began.

SLOW DANCING WITH BILLY

Last night I dreamed you and I were slow dancing
in a wet field in South Dakota,
and that your hair smelled like wheat and was somehow
still long and yellow enough for me to breathe in a dream.
When I woke I wanted to call South Dakota and tell
the operator that when I was fourteen years old
I thought you looked just like Apollo, describe
how you looked walking out of a field of seven-foot
sunflowers with thirteen-inch heads so heavy
it was all they coud do to follow the sun in a day.
Tell her how the dog crept off to the chicken farm
to play tag, how the outhouse blew away in a storm
and when we went to buy another an old man came
to the door and called me your boy. How you ran
your fingers through my short hair and said,
Yes, my beautiful boy.
All day long I kept thinking about that twenty-mile
drive into Aberdeen for a glass of whiskey.
It is fourteen years now since I sat next to you
on a tractor waiting for dark.
Last night when we slow-danced it was all just the same.
Why didn't I marry you?
Why did I take that hostess job in Minneapolis?
We drove out of town and the collected reflections
of cities hit the northern ice caps and a shimmering
curtain of light illuminated the sky over the winter prairie.
Another winter passed and you met some mean girl
in a downtown bar and I started going out with the
motorcyclist and then the musician and at your wedding
your grandma shouted IT WON'T LAST
and then winked at me. At the reception your weeping bride
drove me out the door with her champagne glass
and after that I never saw you again.
When I was eleven I met you and married you in my heart.
It's been twenty-five years and I spent so far this whole day
remembering some dancing we never even did.

FJORDS

FJORDS

My people are known for their depression,
hypersensitivity to rejection and acute awareness of pain.
Many of us, alcoholic.

Each day, a sense of dread.
Life, work, earth and death.
I try to get my bearings.

In my sleep I was clearing tables in Paris.

My people drink coffee all day and are
quiet in public, suspicious.
They prefer to die alone on the ice.

You must eat more fish, my doctor insists.
I prefer a bottle of painkillers, a purple hat,
a paper-bag full of cash and a ticket to a French city.

My ancestors are ice fishermen.
Any one of them could have been eaten by a bear.
I sit before a hole in the ice, line in hand.

Madness, alcoholism and suicide.

My people keep secrets at the cost of coherence.
Tell them something personal, or embarrassing,
they look away, nod, say, Uh Huh.

That's all. Came home one winter night to grandpa
in the kitchen standing at a slant. He named each object
with his finger: peaches, potato, hot water and bread.

A can of beer fell from his pants and pulsed onto the floor.
My people sleep too deeply to awaken. Lie on the couch
drinking whiskey from a Pepsi can, escaping religion and poverty.

I am a realist. I believe in destiny. The world is feudal.
Futile. Foetal. Fatal. Brutal. Total. Half finished.

◆

ARLENE STUCK IN NURSING HOME

She weeps when she sees me. The word she uses is *captive.*
I peer at her from behind three enormous scarlet peonies.
The smell they carry is voluptuous in this dry unlikely hallway.
She is ninety-four. I am forty-two. When I was five she called me *Doll.*

I comb her hair, flat in back like a baby left lying alone too long,
rub balm on her cracking lips. She closes her eyes, tips back her head,
sighs as the wax touch slides over her mouth. I wheel her to the
    elevator,
then outside to the rooftop patio. She inhales the hot summer air, looks
    over my head,
sees the flat bricks of other apartment buildings.

Are those children swimming? They're all dressed in yellow, she tells me.
She talks about the train we're taking home. *Distances come together here.*
She has me in the kitchen, putting on coffee with her mother,
    dead thirty years.
I saw my Joe put into the ground. How is it I see him here,
married to another woman. Can this be real?

I explain how people can look cruelly alike and not be the same.
She nods and pushes at her white hair. *Thank you. I'll remember that.*
She looks into my eyes. *You crawled up out of your deep grave.*
So just sit there and bubble.
She's talking to someone invisible beside me. *Do you need a blanket?*

Do you think he's cold, she asks, *with his chest uncovered?*
When I speak to her it's like breaking into a dream.
This meat thing. Everybody's mad. The children are running away.
We are waiting for a train, I am a friend from another time.
The veil here is so thin she can show me the open grave.

She wants me to push her into the lounge to see her husband and his
    new wife.

Last night, she tells me, *was a rough time downtown.*
We didn't get home until after midnight. She looks up, speculatively,
This is not my ceiling. She looks back at the little boy,
    asks if I think he's cold.
I wouldn't want to sit here and let it blow through my skin.
What, honey? she says to the small, uncovered boy.

Put your head down farther, she tells me, motioning.
    I think she is teaching me to dive.
She watches the children at the seashore of the rooftops.
    Jump in, she says.
I wish I could go with her to this beach and train station
    where the dead swim & wait.
You, she tells me, *have a perplexed look to your character.*
She looks into the breezy shoreline, asks, *Are those cattle real?*

MINNEAPOLIS SUMMER DREAM

When I come to her door she is sleeping. I am getting used to her
    skeletal
appearance. I open her curtains and then the window. She says my
    name.

This breeze, soft as cotton. Straight from heaven. Stretch out,
she commands, and I am glad to. We see a translucent daytime moon.

And I know that everywhere I go now, in my life, the moon will be
    frozen
over the nursing home while we line up on her narrow bed to watch it.

The moon, a tatoo worn inside the eyes.

Soon the nurse will come in to close the window and look at my dress,
how the buttons in back gap at this prone posture, how rough my bare
    feet are.

Arlene and I are real but we are not possible.
We are somewhere between Death and the West.

Here is how we always said goodbye: quickly, lightly,
no tears, no words of farewell. Only "so long" or "next time."

When you leave, she tells me, *you take earth with you.*
Her head drops back on the pillow, delicate bones of the skull.

I think because we have cried together we have said our goodbyes

and she gasps and weeps, *My beautiful loyal friend.*
I have to calm myself. I will imagine that she is sleeping.

She laughed and I saw her name typed inside her mouth.
My eyes watered and my heart struck until I remembered her dentures.

They put her name on things and then they lose them.
She is wearing someone else's clothes, name tags inside.

Life just keeps swishing along.

My mother tells me on the phone
that Arlene is no longer making any sense.

I am holding my good friend's baby in my arms while a second friend
reads her poem about a lover that died.

I am breaking in my chest and cannot breathe and I drown.
I put the baby's blanket over my eyes.

She sleeps on. The friend stops her poem.
None of this will ever be finished. A loss too big to contain.

Death's approach made us lovers too late.

JANUARY

I am zipping shut the coats of the second graders
    and tying shut their hoods
when someone in the same old reindeer sweater
    worn since I met him last September
and boots that smell so strong of cowshit his teacher
    makes him leave them in the hall
comes up behind me slips an arm around my waist
    leans into me then he is gone
and down the hall I hear a teacher yell
    Travis! Where do you belong?

But he is too thin and swift
    slips sideways in the wind
concealed by coloration. Not even a scent of his own yet.
    His brain refuses to process letters.
Mrs. Roberts says he has a cognitive delay
    and will probably do just what his dad does, she says.
Take care of somebody else's cows.
    Travis, slipping rapidly out of sight.

Although my first class is in the kindergarten
    I enter the building through the elementary door
pass the kindergarten and wave at Travis, who is visiting
    his brother and can't wave back because the grey and white rat
is running inside the sleeve of his shirt toward his throat
    and he motions with his face at this movement.
His almond eyes are the color of my brother's before he was lost.
    The color of honey, the eyes of my brother . . .

FEBRUARY

We can't see the galaxies beyond the Milky Way
    says the man on the radio
because we can't see past beauty
    it absorbs the light of our attention.

The souls of animals animate the night sky.
    Children whisper the names of heaven, making them up as they go.
Every fashion, the man goes on to say, embodies a secret, complicated
    wish.

It don't matter, says Travis, dyslexic fifth grader.
    But Travis, I say, it's an observer dependent universe.
Pay attention to the words on the line, in the picture, put
    deer
in the middle of nowhere, by itself, in the spotlight of empty space. Put
    leaps
by itself too. The long mouth of open, the ohh of soul and poem.

He writes: my soul is a rabbit walking inside me. I like when it catches
    my food.
    Not the father's scary home. Not the booze, the silence of the
    mother.
Not the car bodies in the yard but something outside this Ravalli
    County . . .
    Some children look smooth and polished.
Some children look as though they fend entirely for themselves.
    No socks today. No breakfast either.
He's getting his letters confused. Travis, once I forgot the alphabet for a
    whole year.

He will not go bad like bruised fruit.
    He will simply lose interest.
As intricately as binding a foot he is convinced he is worth nothing.
    Peripheral antelope-eyed boy is slipping off the edge.
I have seen you leaning above another child as hopeless as yourself,
    more tender than a mother.

DEAF SCHOOL

Deaf kids laugh
    from the bus stop
        in the rain.
The sound
    comes into my long
        yellow room

pulls me to the window
    to watch
        the tops of their umbrellas

unheard voices rising
    like doves in the airshaft
        on a dull day.

Triumphant
    as the ruby strawberries
        in the deep black garden

or the red fingernails
    that hold the striped umbrella
        whose words sing

like city birds
    flying off her hands
        and up into a tower of air

which is all the light
    some of these rooms get.

MATH POEM

I was audited in 1986 for some unreported waitressing
and I ended up paying six times the original amount.
Yesterday this grim bitch on the phone sluiced through
her teeth the information that I am now being audited
for the two years before that, too, and have to file
immediately for six and seven years ago.
I said I didn't remember where I worked then, or
where I lived. She said she was sending my folder
to Montana and I'd better report to a tax center myself.
I remember that in 1983 I left my crazy husband
and lived way uptown with 4 other women in a building
so run down the city seized it from the owner, making it 7A
which means a sleazy lawyer gets paid to continue
running the place down and sexually harass the female
tenants on top of it. I threw my tax forms away that year.
I made 8,000 dollars and the next year it seems I worked
all the time and lived on the subway. In December I had to move
from the Bronx into a room in Washington Heights. I hope
I did my taxes. I don't know. I read that in Texas an old man
killed himself after his banker Charles Keating "lost"
the old man's life savings while increasing his own
substantial fortune and one of those years I was waitressing
in a place where every day I tied a rag around my hair and
put up all the chairs and mopped the floor after my shift
and the IRS says they've investigated me through friends,
family and employers and they've found more quarters
beneath the dirty plates. I know right now if they push
my mother she'll sing. Today in the mail I got an envelope
it says IRS it has a red line along the bottom like its butt
is bleeding or yours will be once you open the thing.
When I do they tell me in triplicate that I overpaid
some 60 bucks in 1988 and they will be sending it on to me.
It's called intermittent reinforcement/ good cop and psycho cop.
The terrible voice of the woman who called with the news
was the sound of something gnawing on a bone and this
jinx cloud over my head, in the shape of a hand
or a large empty glove falls slowly over my eyes.
I look up, and then I remember, IRS.

MATCHSTICK, HUMMINGBIRD

The next day she is asleep with her mouth open,
breathing like a moth. I sit on the bed and take her hand.
She opens her eyes, says my name.

Groggy, she rubs my upper arm, remarking upon how strong and
    smooth,
how warm my skin.
She sees that I am afraid,

 pulls herself slowly over, grimacing as she moves the broken leg.
"Lie down, Doll," she says, and pats the bed. One railing is up like a
    crib.
I stretch out beside her. We share a pillow. She is a wisp and a husk, all
    eyes.

I wonder for an instant how this looks from the hall.
I don't care how this looks. I want to lie with her until she dies.
I want to put my face to hers and inhale her last breath, pull her into
    me.

"Now rest," she says, feeling my heat against her.
Strings of tears fill my ears and splash onto our pillow.

The only person on earth who can get me to sleep in the day.
When she goes the last layer lifts. There will be nothing over my head.

SALMON EROS

Even the closest are incomprehensibly far
    they say about the stars
while your hands are a pair of calfskin gloves
    palm-up beside the wood stove
in sexual prayer. Soot gathers at the fingertips.
    You are not here.
I sit up in my bed, the fire out, wondering
    if you ever saw more than my reflection
saw my hips and ribs, saw my mouth, saw my life open
    so you could see yourself
inside dreaming your separate dream.
    This town where I sleep is a little traveling carnival on the Idaho
    range,
the bright necklace a child drops into a black lake.
    Where I sit up and feel my soul like water in my mouth.
Where, through a dark room, the naked image
    tries to discern itself in an oval mirror.
I peer into my own likeness, see the dark gesture the body makes,
    the sudden confusion when you have been asleep
and find even the most indelible impression ghostly,
    and not necessarily true.

JULY 4TH QUARTER MOON
SEMICOLON

Horses circle the sky.
Venus hangs above the crescent moon
like a semicolon, a woman's eye
as a jewel and the slip of moon
that is her arm comes to rest
hand on hip.
Behind us the horses have landed.
They watch in silence.
Now, a family climbing
up the mountain lights
sparklers and waves them in circles
imitating the sky
scaring the dogs who run low and whine
while Venus and the moon combine
to suggest a hesitation not as complete
as a stop
or a lounge singer who leans against the night
like it was a piano and winks at us
from her one, good, luminous eye.

3RD WEEK JULY

The third week in July of that last year
when she was still in the nursing home
when we both thought there was a chance
she would ever go home again, wear her own clothes,

lie in her own bed and review her ceiling;
when we played fast and loose with mortality,
making plans together for when she got out;
getting an apartment together, going out for sweet and sour . . .

by then she was already formulating her theories
about how her husband Joe, a decade dead, had turned up in the lunchroom,
staring at her without speaking, wheeling himself to the door
of her room to continue staring in silence . . .

One afternoon I convinced her to roll out to the lounge.
You can meet people, I wheedled, make friends. So there we sat, all of us
in lunch formation mid-afternoon. Dozing and shouting and suspicious and
    drugged
hunched over in wheelchairs, dazed in front of the color t.v . . .

The entertainment lady made popcorn and poured Koolaid into dixie cups.
Arlene tried to give her popcorn to dead Joe, who sometimes did seem to gaze
at her, a drowsy and wordless stare but his real wife waved away the offer.
Arlene shrugged and gripped her cup. She looked at me.

Sometimes she was like a bright bird perched, momentarily . . .
I held my koolaid up in her direction and said Cheers, Arlene
& she raised her eyes & her cup, joie de vivre & a cloud of white hair
while around us every soul slowly lifted a cup into the air

like candles emitting heat and light although they couldn't remember why

or for whom, just that they had once loved that they once had reason to love . . .

CRUEL TEETH OF TRAP

I taught you how to open a house and sweep.
Shake rugs and bring in flowers.

You taught me how to find pitch
in the wood of the tree and start
fire at night in the winter forest.

You taught me to shoot a gun.
How not to entertain a bore.
To hammer. To chop wood.

I gave you my best recipes.
Taught you how to shop for sheets.
Told you about Jung.

You steadied my aim weekends at the dump.
I asked you your dreams
until you began remembering them.

You taught me to lift weights and resist salesmen.
I showed you on alternate Tuesdays how I'd piece
together my personality after a high-impact collision with childhood.

You taught me how to break out of a stranglehold.
How to break a man's wrist with my pencil.
I showed you the secret handshake.

You came from behind and gripped my throat
I scraped and ducked at once like you showed me
broke away from you turned put out your eyes left you in a heap on
    the street.

"Good," you said, getting up, "Again."
You told me not to be afraid to hurt you.

I showed you all of my dangerous edges without the details.
Without plot and description.
Just the bare bones of it.

Just the foot of the animal.

FRIBBLE

Last year at Deaf School
    I got pulled aside and spoken to
        because someone saw him kissing my hand.
Venu's dream: him and me over a strawberry fribble
    in a booth at Friendly's
        arms over each other's shoulders,
old soldiers in this old war.

After dinner and homework we wander the track
    the dorm parent says it's ok. We hold hands and run.
        Venu clutches his imperfect heart,
lifts his head, and laughs like a daredevil
    whose life expectancy is a broken line on a small brown hand.
        In my dreams he makes the sign, *please.*

This year his teacher tells me our behavior is inappropriate.
    Bad do, she signs to Venu.
        Strawberry ice cream I love you, he signs,
from across the lunchroom, drinking his milk
    and humming along, alone at the detention table
        for pointing the wrong finger at his teacher who shrieks.

Venu, I'm married and I'm thirty-eight years old, I sign.
    He signs, *Best sweetheart soon old.*
        Venu, our predicament is older than stone.

THE LAWS OF A NATURE

I can feel the dissolution of my neighbor's marriage across the street.
I thought they were mad at me their basement was full
the forgotten stuff was like a canyon I could hardly breath in that house
then one day over the fence she told me.
    I didn't tell her I had known all along.
There are strict laws that apply to all of us for example

the roofers working on the house across the street watch me.
A pile of dresses and rags tossed down becomes a peripheral child
I think the workmen dislike me because I talk to dogs
and work on a laptop computer here in the yard like a millionaire
a cordless phone on the bench beside me just a small

woman if I was born in India however set on fire
over a dowry or had my nose cut off by a jealous husband in Pakistan...
meanwhile the governor of Minnesota
spoke at a convention my mother was waitressing that night
    she told me that he said
we have turned the tide of public opinion against smoking
    now we must stop the battering of women.
She was glad it was a smoke-free room she was working.

I can sit in my yard with the spaniels and use a laptop and wonder about the
    law of diminishing returns.
Shouldn't we expect as many surprises and miracles as we have seen already?
My friend saw the first automobile and t.v. set, penicillin and the atom,
    test-tube baby, cloned sheep, man on the moon.
Soon I will take these miracles in stride, curse them for their slowness.
    Assume

someday the sun powers everything imagine
    an algae that sucks up an oil spill
imagine the world in the eye of a goose while I am here queen of the yard
imagining a bee has gotten entangled in my hair it is the focus of my being
the roofers climb down and drive home the bee is incensed my phone rings
the dog across the street blinks at me in surprise.

I worry about my mother going to park her car downtown
    in an underground ramp.
First parking structure built here in my town
    and immediately a woman is raped in it.
Guy came to the house
    I like an idiot opened the door he grabbed my forearms
pushed me toward the back of the house those two lazy dogs
    sprung from nowhere
didn't make a sound made for his throat
    two airborne missiles of fur

the guy ran off down the street
    I called the police tried not to imagine.
Now my friend who saw the first car is ninety-four
    and her bones are breaking
her kids put her in a nice nursing home nice yes it's clean nice
    it's peaceful no pee smell
she's alone in a bland room she says,
    "this is not my ceiling."
People who work there make minimum wage how can I get them to
    love her
they put her on Zoloft, she weighs eighty pounds, takes only aspirin
suddenly she's groggy all the time sleeping away with her mouth gaping
just like all the others—a line of skeletons tied into wheelchairs stoned
into a passive pre-death now she's losing her grip
dis-associating talking with the dead looking over our heads and
    nodding
after all she's been in the world—to this?

my mother and her sister Donna live on both sides of my friend,
did her shopping and wrote her checks. They went in on a microwave at
Xmas so she could heat the meals they dropped off
before her eyes got bad she was a seamstress she
sewed from French Vogue patterns when she made me a skirt
she'd say, now wear heels and feature your legs

and for one suit she made she asked me to wear a bra
    to do her darts justice
but don't worry about a girdle, she said, patting me
    up and down all over.

Now she can't find her mouth with her spoon.
    A different guy indifferently dresses her every morning.
When I call they say she's not available but they take a message.
    Do they tell her I love her every time?
She doesn't remember anyone saying that.

Governor Arnie Carlson is going to try to get men
    to stop battering women.
I am going to try to get my friend
    out of the nursing home where she is captive.
The roofers are going to try to finish today and go home.
The future will surprise us in ways we can't imagine.
The neighbors will probably divorce.

SAWTOOTH RANGE & PAHSIMEROI VALLEY

Over the sound of the river, the whispers of the parents,
  the bawling of cows from the horizon,
over the high mountain desert as red as Mars
  over the conversations of the living and the murmur
at the edge of the twentieth century

  I lie on a cot in a log cabin looking out a window
into the dark extension with its rare, scattered lights
  glimmering from long-dead stars and mercury vapor lamps.
My grandmother died in childbirth at age thirty.
  I feel her struggle against the denial of time inside my cells.

I feel the goddess Nut stretching to reach the milk star.
  I feel the desire of things to break from their shapes.
Walking along a dirt road in the Sawtooth Mountains
  I am afraid, as always, of the indefinite object.
I make the echoing EEE YAAA of the Thai pig-calling women.

  Frightening fright. No wildcat, no mad skunk, no bear.
No badger, wolf, wolverine, no wild dog.
  A blue truck approaches. Two bearded men, rifles
hanging in the gun rack. I stand beside the road clutching a rock.
  Squinting into the sun, I wait for the men to determine history.

I always ask the children to write about animals.
  After a few weeks in this area I stop asking.
I am tired of stories of cruelty, neglect, murder.
  Do animals have feelings? I ask my classes.
Does an animal have a soul? But they do not, most of them, know soul.

I ask the rancher's wife why the herd of cows I hear
  from the horizon has been bawling with grief all week.
They're being weaned from their calves, she says.
  They sound sad, I say.
Yes, she says, they seem to feel sorrow.

  The wild grasses here, they say, used to grow high as a horse's belly.
All the wild grass, gone.

MY DREAM / P.S. 152
Class Collaboration / 4th Grade / South Bronx

My Dream.
    I am being chased by a roach/my mother's boyfriend/hunger
big vegetables/the cops.
    Along came a mouse on a motorcycle and got big and big
and grabbed me and saved me.
    I had a packet of oreo cookies and some milk
the puppet came and punched me I body-slammed him
      against the wall, broke open his head
my mother came home from work it was only a bad dream.

My Dream
    was that the coconut man was dancing with me
I was a ninja and the movie was the return of the living brains
    and I crawled up out of the oreo cookie and the hunter shot me.
My mother woke me up I was on the couch it was not real.

I Dreamt
    that my mother's boyfriend from a long time ago came back.
He is so kind. He gives me presents, takes me places. A beautiful car.
    I don't care that he . . .
Just that he loves me.
    I was hiding and it came up out of the basement, out of its grave
and the king came and kissed me on the lips.
    My head was broke. The mouse came on the motorcycle
with the dragon and Mr. T and my mother came home from work
and I was locked out and I woke up in Bumland, Whiskey River,
    Rum and Coca-Cola Forest, Bad Breath Monster,

and then I flew away.

RINGFINGER

I was having lunch
with some ranchers.
I noticed no one was wearing a ring.
Louie, on my left, connected
with a live battery beneath
the hood of a truck once
and took his off forever.
Guy on my right jumped lightly
from a beam and hung himself,
ringfinger, to a nail.
Full weight, three feet from the ground.
Man across the table had butcher's hands,
color of raw meat, knuckles
the size of walnuts.
One finger doesn't move at all.
"Ya reach into the machinery," he says, "& bang!"

Then I tell them how my ring
caught me up in a marriage
where I hung, afraid to fall,
for years.

Felt it deep up into my armpit, he said.

When it happened
we thought the ring
would tear our hearts out.

SALMON, IDAHO PERSEPHONE

I bump into Maria at the nectarines.
We both squeeze what does not give
in hopes of spring.

She selects and then replaces a yellow peach
with fiery cheeks.
"I just keep thinking about her
getting away from the old man," she says.

We sidle to seedless grapes, keeping an eye out for
pomegranates, hawks, flowers that appear
from a crack in the floor.

Large hands, dented cans, bruised fruit
grain fruit seedy fruit snakes skin
& chariots.

Spring is coming. I feel her
feel his grip loosening.

NOTHING TO FEAR

At age five I landed in the back yard beside her;

already a ruined woman of a child.
I think too much and I feel even more, I want a rest

from these nerves. Like piles of leaves
in a slight wind, they whip themselves into an exhausted dishevel.

A child runs through them, and then a dog, thrash, and scatter.

I see her in the faces of newborns. I wait in my dream on her front
    lawn.
I know her house has been gutted. Disassembled, like the oldest
    woman.

When she slept I crept into her room where the picture hung of the
    children
jumping off the dock into the lake. I could never be sure she was alive.

Arlene your gardens lie beneath the old walls, the ruins of our
    kingdom.
Nothing to fear. That is what we told each other.

I could see death's smile in hers.
I tried to see her as a stranger would, so that I could teach strangers to
    love her.

I had so little time. There was a delicate Somali man who once brushed
her hair. She had a dream the nurse's aid ate all the chocolate.

Her earrings weren't missing, they were sold.
Every article in that house sold on the first day. That which was never

born never dies, swings both ways timewise through the
promiscuity of death like a wedding dance. Babysbreath. Feverfew.
    Moss rose.

Even now she applies for rebirth and finds it no easier than dying.
Lilac. Stone bird bath. Little Skipper barking in the shadow.

LOVE, SLEEP & PARIS

IDAHO VOLLEYBALL TEAM

Once I was up at this hot springs resort in Idaho
    when suddenly a girls' volleyball team and two coaches
        came whooping and pushing from the dressing rooms.

To get an idea of this place, think of a giant Roman spa,
    fat grandmothers floating among kids and pool toys and teenagers.
        In my memory high vaulted ceilings arch to cathedral windows,

open skylights where flocks of doves wheel and call.
    I can't be sure of this, but I do know there's an atmosphere of higher living
        where sparkling plates of broken water reflect onto us like jewelry.

Then these coaches came out, rancher types,
    with tender feet that never see the sun.
        Onto the cold cement floor and into the pools

wearing black socks with their bathing suits.
    Into the pool of screaming teenage ranch girls
        with big voices and athletic shoulders

fighting through each other to dunk the coaches,
    deafening us with great echoing voices.
        Aggressive, animal-loving, self confident.

I was sitting on the deck, worrying about the skin on my thighs.
    I saw myself fallen away from the pool of girls,
        into early sophistication, isolation, and the desire to be very small.

Remember the ones you loved best, their hair swinging behind them,
    pounding against the earth, beating their own best time.
        What I love about those girls is what I loved about myself

before I stilled my running girl, the larger self that I swallowed
    like a twin born with another twin inside her,
        when only one can live.

FUR COAT

After she died he quit shaving.
When we met, mornings, to walk the dogs
I could smell liquor on his breath.
He was smoking again and spoke
in a careless voice like a rougher man.

One morning he gave me her gold compact,
three beaded evening bags and a mink pillbox hat.
"Do you like to go out at night?" he asked.
"Get dolled up?"
"Sometimes," I answered, peering into the small mirror
in my hand, forest canopy framing my head.

Finally he gave me her fur coat.
Told me this story: when he was a young salesman
she traveled with him in the car. Sometimes when
she got tired, bored of the road, they stopped
at a hotel and she put the coat on with nothing beneath it.

On a hot August day I carried the coat to my car.
In my shadowy bedroom I put my hands in the pockets,
looked in the mirror and saw something in my own eyes.
Felt her stir. Put the half-stick of chewing gum in my mouth.
I could smell her powder. I was almost two women.

She played bridge and read detective novels.
Smoked in bed. Wore long hostess gowns, had her hair
done downtown. When she fell in the kitchen she never told him.
Blacked out at the mall. Her birthday came, then the diagnosis.

Once he told me his nightmare. He is shooting coyotes
from a helicopter. His dog falls out, lands amid
the swirling pack, and disappears.
"Rowdy," he cries, sitting bolt up, "come back."

CAT CALL

Last night, he tells me,
I called out in my sleep for Steve.

You groaned, he said, and it woke me.
A cat screamed out back.

You sounded surprised, he tells me, when you said it.
The dogs became excited. He got up and closed the window.

Who is this guy? he asks at breakfast.
At my hair in the mirror I wonder.

What about that cat calling off Mt. Jumbo to our house.
There was a name in my mouth from that other life.

What was I going to tell Steve when my husband interrupted?
Eyes of darkness fill like pools when I lie down.

A stranger comes out of me.
I call him back.

I cannot open this window.

OUR GHOST, MRS. THOMPSON

We had a ghost in our house for a few years,
    turning on lights and exciting the dogs.
In a phone call from the old owner we were able to learn her name.
    She lived here for her lifetime, fell in the hall and died.
When the old owners argued she slammed doors
    dropped drawers of silverware and threw the broom.
Made noises from the bottom of the basement stairs.
    They divorced, sold the house and moved away.
Our dogs jumped up, barking. The porch light came on and striped our bed.
    My husband got up and stood in the hallway.
Are you lonely? he asked. Are you afraid? She held very still.
    Held the breath of the house in her mouth.
After a while even the dogs seemed to like her.
    My husband told me, She's afraid of the dark.
We still have her kitchen clock, her ironing board, its linen slipcover.
    When I press our shirts steam rises in a gentle old air.
Don't be afraid. Funny when she locked us out, hooking the screen doors
    from the inside. And when I put botanical wallpaper in the kitchen
we found her medicine chest in the shed lined with my new paper.
    Don't be afraid. Grandmother breathes and lights flicker.
She informs us of the other world, the alley between.
    You can always lead from any one dream to the secret thought.
And so ghosts work. Come back. We aren't afraid. We miss you.

ANY AMOUNT OF CRICKETS

I could be any woman in the world
and you
any man.
This bed, iron in a nearly naked room
this bed, and a window
where the light leaks in against all my best effort
could be
anybody's bed.

Outside a field of how many yellow
and then blue somethings.
In this shell of air I hear
the ocean in the freeway.
A man standing deep in waves swings his long hair
in an arc. In our eyes
drops of water fly like new stars.

Constellations are born in the most casual gesture.
Any amount of breathing
any amount of crickets chittering
any two people whose hearts line up
anywhere
lie down together
sky overhead
night tossing like a sleepless mind.
This world, how we think
we have it memorized.

KUNDALINI

Last night as we lay curled together
in that place, reverie,
we felt a current of electricity
pass between us.
Did you feel that? I asked.
Yes, he said, I sure did.
It came from you, I told him, and moved up my spine.
No, he said, it came from you. It went into my thighs.
Kundalini? I wondered, snake in spine uncurling?
I lie awake and imagined the stars through the ceiling.
The little dog crept up to sleep beside me.
Honey, I whispered, I think it's a good sign.
But he was dreaming, said, *Oh, oh, oh.*
He had already gone ahead of me into that dark country.

ASLEEP, PARIS

1.
I am standing in the streets of the Left Bank in Paris
watching the refugees paint a mural across the sides of
several buildings. It is called, The Exodus of Kabul
and to look at it makes you want to weep. Beside me
my friend wears black leather and sports a butterfly
tatoo on his throat. He reaches his arm behind me
and without touching me touches me deeply.
I am watching the movement of the colors, from the
stream of Afghani people out of the mural into Paris.
I look at the street signs and the buildings, the activity
of the Parisians and I say the same thing to myself
that I say each of these nights in Paris—
Memorize Everything.

2.
I get a job in a bistro where I haul buckets
up huge stone steps from the basement.
I am a spectacular busgirl. Soon I am promoted to
hostess. I sashay table to table and never forget a
face. As my French improves I take reservations
over the phone. I do numbers, dates, last names.
I wake up in the morning repeating the days of the week.

3.
I find a hotel that will rent me a bureau drawer to sleep
 inside and that is my room. It tucks away. In the day
I can walk Paris memorizing street signs. I have a vague
concern that my flight home has left.

4.
I sit at a table with an old lover and two women.
As dusk approaches the women pull long black scarves over their hair
& then the sky, too, is black. I awaken, saying, I will get a scarf.
In one gesture I will pull the sky across my hair.

5.
I have a felt hat with two brims. It is the same purple as my lipstick.
I sit in a bar called La Pêche. The bartender winks at me.
I wink back at myself in the mirror. In my hand I hold
a brown paper bag full of cash. *This time, Paris . . .*
I step into the bathroom and wash my bare feet in the sink.

6.
Outside it's raining. I see the bar's name in pink neon.
I look up into the dark Paris night and say, *impermeable.*
There is a man at a cash machine who wears a brown hat and
trench coat. He is entirely familiar. Happily, I walk toward him.

7.
I look up *pêche* in my French dictionary. Sometimes
it means peach, sometimes sin and it can also mean fish.
I look up impermeable. It means raincoat.
Party of two, Thursday evening, eight o'clock. Springtime. Here with me,
asleep, in Paris.

MAP COMMENTARY

In dreams, you are everyone.
Except for the dead, they are always themselves.

—Bethard's Dream Book

1.
She used to say we would last forever.
She used to say we were *a going thing.*
She came back, briefly, with a map
The land was bright green, the coast unsteady.
It was drawn in crayola on a piece of cardboard.
She pointed to her country, then to mine.
Attached to the flesh in the karma of female birth;
now separated by a single body of water.
One which she has already swam across,
one I wait in line to swim.

2.
Did I say how bright the colors were? How clumsy the hand . . .
Specifics on this map are the kind of thing
you can't look at directly; like an eclipse or angry dog.
Something you glance away from and observe sidelong.
There was no north or south. She said something about the volume,
how there was no control. This bothered her greatly.
She asked me to do something about it.
Once she said she would always be with me;
even after death. "I won't bother you," she said,
"but when you need to make a decision you'll feel I'm there."
If you turned the coardboard map in another direction, all bets were
off.
No X for treasure, no symbolic key to guide you.
I suggested we go for a ride in her car.
Ruby and Esther wouldn't let her. "Come back dearie," they said,
pulling her into the dark. She covered her ears. "Do something," she
mouthed.
I fiddled with some dials. I wanted to ask her something but she was
gone.

THE FIRST AFTERLIFE ARLENE DREAM

I am walking
up the front stairs to my parents' house.
I look next door at her white stucco house; it is exactly the same but
empty now.
I see someone has left Arlene's Bible in the dirt beneath some bushes.
I recognize that she has left it there for me.
I never get to see her face, hear her words, the way
she used to gasp over the phone, long distance, when
she heard me say my name, the way
she made over some of her dresses for me
when all of my clothes were lost
in the fire of my
adolescence.

FILAMENTS, TENDRILS & RUNNERS

My husband blooms against my skin.
    Something fearless in me
        starts beating time.
            Not the hands of the uncle who died drunk.
Once a man on an airplane
    told me he'd had a silent stroke
        doctors discovered new veins
            migrating from the unhurt side of his brain.
From the French for tender
    tendrils reached his injury
        drew a new map of blood.
Sexuality a wild tree
    springing from the char.
        I dream I am a house.
            Climb the stairs and lie on the floor.
My hips grow into the wood.
    I can walk all night
        without stopping
            and never enter all the rooms.
The books fall from their sleeves and the mirrors
    move like water. Other women move in these hallways.
        There are secret staircases and clothes that fit me.
        I stand smiling with friends
            in the photographs.
Sometimes I can read the words in their open books.
    Sometimes I am writing the books.
        The bed cries out in my voice, Don't!
            I am my own house I have some ghosts we
              don't bother each other.
Meantime, dreamtime, everyone else bailed out of the plane.
    We hung in low branches and the other passengers
        jumped into the streets and ran.
All night I moved in circles above a black ocean.
    Was green, a triangle moving forward by turning inside out.
        I landed in Orly Airport, found a room and a job
        bussing tables at a bistro.

I carry water from the basement in buckets.
        Coins fall from my apron. Ink in the pens turns to milk.
             Water turns to wine. I've lost my limp. I rarely scream.
         I am working on my French.
He touches me, smelling of moss, tobacco and talcum.
        He blooms against my skin. Tendrils reach everywhere.
      I'm a living jardin.

POSTSCRIPT

When my father called with the news of your death, Arlene
    I knew as soon as he drew his first breath
        that you had escaped the prison house of your body.

My friend says she can tell that you are inside me now
    like a bead of yellow light, an amber syrup, a pocket of snowfall.
        I am your work. I am the fabric on the dressmaker's form
        you sized to fit me,

pale summer dress with scalloped edges, fur-lined wool cape, brown suit
    with a blouse of roses to accept my award from the president,
        which hadn't come about yet but you insisted it would.

Black and white linen a-line with front pleat that I wore in New Orleans where
    I called you to describe the ships in the gulf I could see from my room.
        Your effect on me runs upward in a chimney of flame,

a river of stone, the sound of curtains sighing in a window.
    The sign of your hand is all over me. I look now like you did
        in nineteen forty,
            or at least I like to pretend I do.
            I am your work.

Your signature is everywhere, like Evening in Paris perfume, like dahlias and
    grand old ladies that keep growing more impossibly beautiful
        as they age; what your hands could do!
        You could've raised a nation.

Instead you chose me, that afternoon in the summer before I turned five.
    I thought you might be Lucille Ball, you were already that fantastic.
    You gave your dog cookies held in your teeth.

I watched your kitchen light from my bedroom window before I slept.
    The flame of your white hair at the table where you sat
        writing serious intelligent letters signed only in your last name.

you said I was simply *a free spirit,* you gave me those words
to change my identity with, a life bigger than anyone else could allow.
Kiddo, you said, *Listen, Doll, you're just like me.*

ORPHEUS

So full of you I had to
lie down in the golden
grass with the sun
coming full off the horizon.

My hips, attached to the earth.
The dogs, above me, licking
each other's faces. My hands,
your hands. I lie upon the ground
to take your weight.

A sky full of honey, suspended & molten.
The yellow, yellow grass waved over my head
like a lion. The wind made a rustling sound.
You were behind me.

Eurydice, I know the law.
I never looked at you.
I closed my eyes, lay down, and opened my long coat.

TELEGRAM

Dear Arlene
    When you died they emptied your house stop
No one wanted your old photos and schoolgirl's notebooks stop
fragile yellowed paper carefully preserved in a suede book stop
The telegram from San Francisco, 1922, which describes
the need for you to come help your sick cousin with her children stop
go to plays and operas stop
I continue paging through until the response from your father, Souix City
Iowa stop explaining that you are too young to make such an agreement
stop you are wanted at home
your father stopped you from leaving home
        he wanted you to learn a trade stop 1922
                was not a good year for a young woman to travel alone stop
You never complained about it you bided your time took
        shorthand classes stop
When you cut off your waist-length auburn hair stop your father wept
The man you came to love did not love you stop
you told me how you kept loving him
stop for the next ten years stop you said it was a pain
stop you lived with stop until
one morning stop you woke up free from this love free to go on
stop sixty years later you told me to look
under the calender pinned to the bulletin board
stop there was a photograph of a man who seems less than remarkable
stop yet you kept his likeness throughout your marriage into old age
stop another of the surprises you kept springing on me
I asked you about love and bitterness stop
asked you what I'd remember most
Asked about success and what that meant stop you dozed beside me
Brittle as a winter garden stop you moved your mouth I put my ear close to
hear you
saying *it only matters that one has loved* stop *not even been loved back* stop *only*
that one has loved stop *and not stopped.*

ZOE MOU SAGAPO

the dog's soft green blanket on the front porch beneath my bare feet
the white blouse that buttons up the back
the insistent air of summer inside the dark shed
the long slow breathing beside me every night of my life
the purple iris and the sudden yellow in the middle of the garden
zoe mou sagapo the black bear and her cub on the edge of our civilization
zoe mou sagapo knowing the Greek words and hearing them roll
from my mind onto my lips the blue eyes of my husband his sturdy legs his
    deep chest
when I look at the world he is the part of it where I flow into the spirit
zoe mou sagapo I whispered to Arlene as she lay waiting to die
    zoe mou sagapo
inscribed inside the circle of his wedding ring saying my life I love you
my life I love you the neighbor on his porch with his cigarette calling hello
the sound of the creek my life my life I love you I love the sound of sleep all of
    us breathing
in the dark together my life I love you the flickering shadows of trees
    falling across the walls
putting the hard light onto the bowl the basket the dishes the sound of the
    water
sprinkling across the lawn the smell of water my life I love you (zoe mou
    sagapo)
the way the black shadows of the lilac trees came in through the screen window
in the cool stone house the brown cotton fabric of the quilt on the bed
made by the father before he died we sat together in a café that day
I ate both our breakfasts my life sagapo when the headache is gone
    my life I love
when she comes into my dreams from death and is real and is herself
the brown cotton sheets my feet still cold from the grass when I watered the
    yard
the children who wave from the schoolbus the sound of my name on the play-
    ground
where they call like sea gulls round the tether ball and on the swings,
and running and running my life my life running and calling
the deep green at night with black at the center
my life zoe mou my life zoe mou when the headache is gone
and the old poet says *I believe in synchronicity* and then he tells me
something about buddha zoe mou zoe I love my life I love

Acknowledgements

Grateful acknowledgement is made to the following magazines and anthologies in which certain of these poems appeared:

Montana Writers Daybook: Fur Coat
Jumbo Love Cycle (CD): Orpheus, Cat Call, Any Amount of Crickets
Intermountain Woman: Donna
United States of Poetry: Goodwill Thrift Store, Missoula
McGraw-Hill-Poetry, Literature and the Essay, Vol. 3: Cruel Teeth of Trap
Exquisite Corpse: Math Poem
McGraw Hill Contemporary Anthology of Poetry: Slow Dancing with Billy
Northern Lights: Salmon, Idaho Persephone; Decade
Women's Literature Quarterly: My Dream P.S. 152
Hubub: July 4th Quarter Moon Semicolon
Wordsmith: Passion
New Rivers Press Best of Twenty-Five Years Anthology: Fribble
Northern Lights New Writing From the American West: Ringfinger
Cutbank: Three True Accounts, The Loneliness of My Brother, Best Seen from a Dark Country Place
Teacup: January, February

I would like to thank The National Endowment for The Arts for a Fellowship which aided in the composition of these poems.

Also thanks to the Montana Arts Council for the 1998–99 Literature Fellowship awarded for the series of Arlene Poems.

I owe so much to the following people; with deep gratitude and profound thanks to Nancy Larson Shapiro, Steve Shapiro, Chris Edgar, Susan O'Connor, Sandra Alcosser, Patricia Goedicke, Kim Anderson, Zan Bockes, Rosellen Brown, B.J. Buckley, Julie Cook, Ed Lahey, Beth Ferris, Mark Gibbons, Judith Johnson, Carolyn Kizer, Deirdre McNamer, Mary Liz Riddle, and Linda Wojtowick.

Photo: Robert Jamshid Rajala

SHERYL NOETHE grew up in Minnesota, then migrated to New York, Paris, Idaho, and Montana. In 1984 she won the Poetry On Stage competition at The Loft in Minneapolis as well as the McKnight Prize for Literature, and New Rivers Press published her first books of poems, *The Descent of Heaven Over the Lake*. For a decade Noethe was a writer-in-the-schools for Teachers & Writers Collaborative in New York City and in Idaho; with Jack Collom, she wrote *Poetry Everywhere*, a guide to teaching poetry published by Teachers & Writers. A poet-in-residence at the New York School for the Deaf for nine years, she continues to teach sign language and use sign in her poetry classes. After serving as a Scholar-in-the-Schools in small towns throughout Montana for the Montana Committee for the Humanities, Noethe helped establish the Missoula Writing Collaborative, where she is the Artistic Director. She continues to teach poetry in schools and community sites and is on the visiting faculty of the University of Montana. Her awards include Fellowships in Literature from the National Endowment for the Arts in 1989 and from the Montana State Arts Council in 1999. Her poems are widely anthologized, and she recorded a CD, *Jumbo Love Cycle*, as part of an effort to preserve her backyard treasure, Mount Jumbo, which she climbs daily with her husband, fireman Robert Rajala, and their two great dogs.